LAURA
AND OLD LUMBER

Sarah Harrison

Illustrated by Kate Aldous

Hutchins

London Melbourne Auck

Laura lived with her father and mother and her younger brother Edmund, at the end house in the village of Lark Rise.

In the back garden was the pigsty where the Dinner Pig lived. I should really have mentioned him at the top of this page, for he was a pig of great importance. Laura's father paid regular visits to the pigsty, and would gaze in at the door for hours. And when other men came to call they would cluster round the sty, scratching the Dinner Pig, and making admiring remarks.

Laura and Edmund shared a bedroom upstairs. The bedroom was cosy and neat, but there was one thing Laura did not like about it, and that was the cupboard in the corner. This cupboard was always kept locked. No one could unlock it, because the key belonged to Mrs Herring, who owned the end house, but who did not live in Lark Rise.

"Why would a cupboard be locked all the time," Laura asked Edmund, "unless there was something nasty in it?"

"I don't know what you're fussing about," replied Edmund loftily. "It's only an old cupboard."

"But what's *inside* it?" Laura wanted to know. Edmund shrugged, and examined his boots.

"It must be something horrible," quavered Laura.

"Then it's just as well it's locked!" declared Edmund in triumph.

It was at night that Laura was most afraid of the cupboard. In the dark, the rest of the room was a fuzzy grey, with the blacker shapes of things that Laura recognised showing through the gloom.

But in the far corner where the cupboard should have been there was only a deep and mysterious blackness which seemed to stare back at Laura like a giant's eye. Laura didn't like to turn her back on the cupboard-eye, and sometimes she would be stiff all over by the time she fell asleep, from lying in one position.

One day, Laura asked her mother about the cupboard. Laura's mother was busy as usual, scrubbing the grate ferociously, with the tip of her tongue sticking out, and her eyebrows pulled together.

"Mother," said Laura casually. "What's in that old cupboard in our bedroom?" Laura's mother kneeled up and blew at the wisp of hair that had fallen on her forehead.

"Whatever makes you ask that?" she said with a smile.

"I mean – why is it always locked?"

"Because Mrs Herring has the key," replied Laura's mother, beginning to scrub once more. "And as to what's in it, just old lumber I shouldn't be surprised, taking up good house space!"

Laura thought Old Lumber sounded suspiciously like a dark and ugly giant with a single staring eye . . .

She went out into the back garden to have a word with the Dinner Pig. She could just see into the sty if she stood on tiptoe with her nose resting on top of the door. The Dinner Pig stretched his nose up towards hers. His big ears hung over his wise and beady eyes like the corners of the starched table cloth which Laura's mother got out for visitors' tea.

"Tell me," asked Laura confidentially, "what do you think of Old Lumber?"

"Grunt, snuffle," said the Dinner Pig, and shook his head.

"No," said Laura, "I don't like the sound of him either."

"Snort!" exclaimed the Dinner Pig.

"Thank you," said Laura politely. "I'm glad you feel the same."

That night, very late, when the whole of Lark Rise was asleep, Laura woke up with a start. There was a rustle . . . then a rattle . . . something was moving in the cupboard in the corner! Quick as a flash, Laura pulled the bedclothes over her head. She could hear her heart beating, like the footsteps of Old Lumber himself.

But after a minute, when nothing more happened, Laura uncurled and poked her head very, very gingerly over the edge of the sheet.

"Edmund!" she whispered. It was a squeaky whisper, like the sound the schoolteacher made when she wiped the

blackboard with a damp cloth. "Edmund, wake up!"

At that moment there was another, much louder noise from inside the cupboard, a thudding and a bumping as if something – or someone – was trying to get out.

"HELP!" screamed Laura. "EDMUND!"

But before Edmund had as much as turned over, Laura's mother came in, looking like a rather cross ghost in her long white nightdress, with her brown hair in a plait over her shoulder, and a candle in her hand.

"Whatever's all this about?" she asked. Laura pointed shakily at the cupboard. "There was an awful noise in there!"

"Hm," said her mother. Fearlessly, she went over to the cupboard and jiggled the handle. "That old lumber wants to come out!"

Laura shivered. It was exactly as she'd feared.

"Now then, miss," said her mother, tucking Laura in firmly so that the mattress jumped, "you go back to sleep. I'll write to Mrs Herring, and ask her to come and sort it out."

The next day, on the way to school, Laura said to Edmund:

"You see, I was right. There *is* something nasty in that cupboard, and Mrs Herring is coming to see to it."

Edmund just charged off to scuffle with the other boys, but Laura could tell he was eaten up with curiosity. Some time went by, and there were no more noises from the cupboard. Then one Sunday Laura's mother was up extra early and baking cakes.

"Tidy that room of yours," she said to Laura and Edmund. "Mr and Mrs Herring are coming today."

"Visitors, is it," said Laura's father, and went out with a glum face to inspect the pig.

All day there were preparations for the Herrings, and a special tea was laid on the table, as was only proper for one about to do battle with an ogre.

But when they arrived, the Herrings were not at all what Laura had expected. Both of them were small, and Mrs Herring herself was a pinched, finicky sort of person, with a beaded bonnet and a disapproving expression.

"What do you think?" mouthed Laura to Edmund as they followed their mother and Mrs Herring up the stairs.

Edmund pulled a face.

In the bedroom, Mrs Herring put her skinny hand, in its black lace mitten, into her small bag, and drew out a long, rusty key.

Mrs Herring put the key in the lock and turned it with a rasping sound.

Laura held her breath.

Slowly, the door creaked open.

Laura took a step backwards.

And with a bang, and a cloud of dust, Old Lumber fell out on to the floor.

Laura's mouth gaped wide enough to catch flies. Where was the horrible, one-eyed, staring giant?

What lay at Mrs Herring's feet was big and black and ugly, all right. But it was a trunk! An old and battered cabin trunk, covered with peeling labels like dead skin. It lay on its side, and the leather straps which held the lid in place were almost worn through.

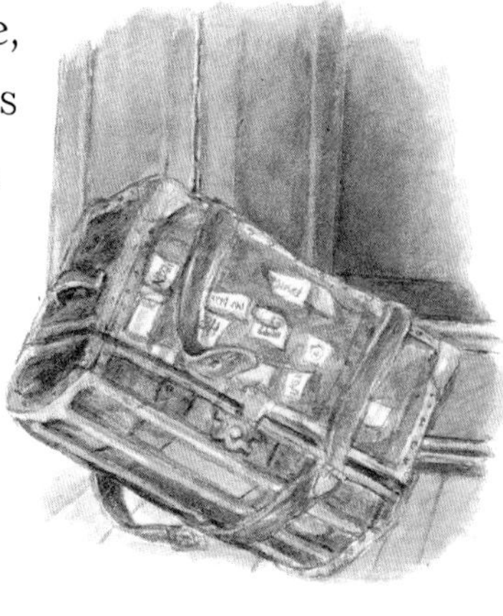

All of a sudden there was a scuffling and a banging, the lid of the trunk flopped open, and the contents of the trunk tumbled out. There was a cracked teapot; an umbrella stand; an assortment of bent knives and forks tied up with string; a box of dog-eared books; a chipped walking stick with a goose's head handle; a dented brass fender; a birdcage; and a pile of dusty old clothes.

And then, as the dust began to settle, something else appeared. And it was most certainly the cause of all the trouble.

Perched on the crown of an old black straw hat, with its whiskers whiffling and its tiny paws held beneath its chin, was a little grey mouse.

The mouse stared around at Laura, and at Laura's mother, and at Edmund, and at Mrs Herring.

And then Mrs Herring gave a shrill scream, and clutched her black skirts tight around her legs, so as to show her bony ankles in wrinkled stockings.

"A mouse!" she shrieked. "Get the horrid thing away from me!" Which was quite unnecessary, for it whisked its tail and disappeared beneath Edmund's bed.

Laura's mother pressed her lips together severely, in a way that meant she was trying not to smile. "Run along now," she said to Laura and Edmund. "And let Mrs Herring get on."

Laura trailed down the stairs, ignoring Edmund's grin. She was dreadfully disappointed.

When Mrs Herring had sorted out the lumber, she gave Edmund a broken corkscrew and Laura a needlecase full of rusty needles, and they all went down to tea. Mrs Herring took very tiny mouthfuls, and chewed everything a thousand times, but Laura noticed that Mr Herring went straight into the cake, without eating bread and butter first as he should have done.

After tea the Herrings loaded the stuff on to their cart and drove away Laura's mother smoothed her hair, and remarked: "Good riddance!"

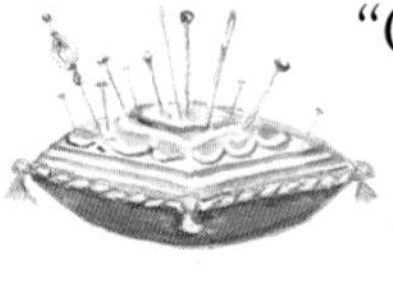

Laura feeling a little foolish, went out to see the Dinner Pig,

"Well," she said. "I was certainly wrong about *that*."

"It was just a lot of old junk in that cupboard, and a little mouse scuttling about."

The Dinner Pig gazed at Laura with his small, beady, knowing eyes.

"Oink!" he said. Just exactly as if he'd known all along.